HOW TO MAKE A MEMORY

Written by

Elaine Vickers

Illustrated by

Ana Aranda

A Paula Wiseman Book

SIMON & SCHUSTER BOOKS FOR YOUNG READERS

New York London Toronto Sydney New Delhi

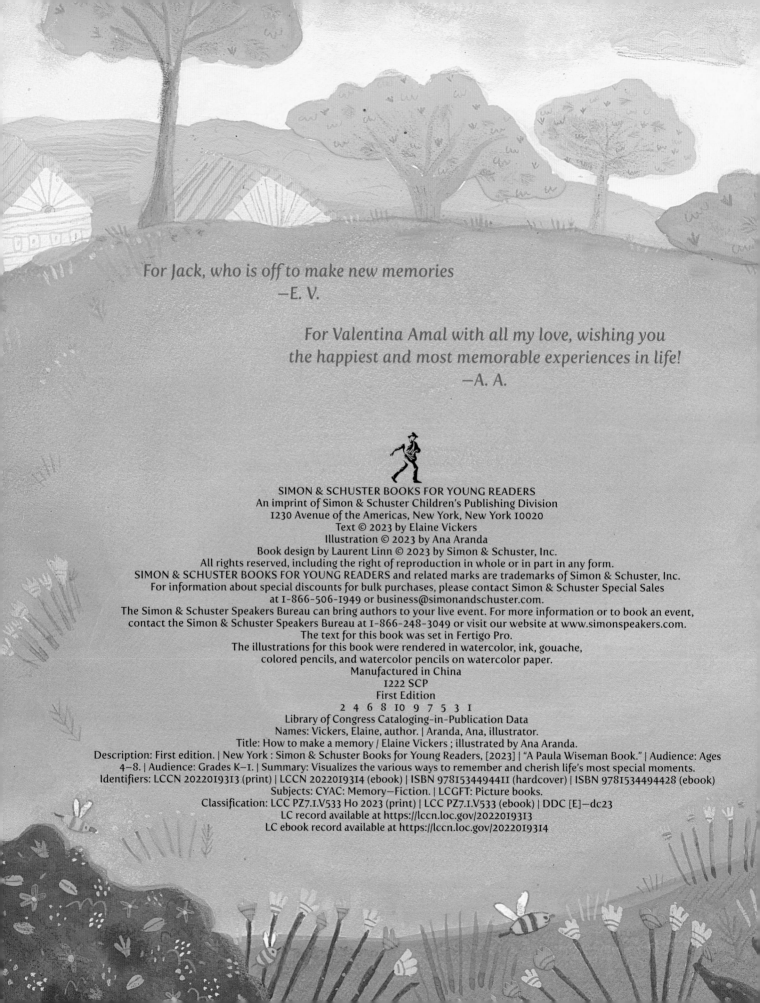

For Jack, who is off to make new memories
—E. V.

For Valentina Amal with all my love, wishing you
the happiest and most memorable experiences in life!
—A. A.

SIMON & SCHUSTER BOOKS FOR YOUNG READERS
An imprint of Simon & Schuster Children's Publishing Division
1230 Avenue of the Americas, New York, New York 10020
Text © 2023 by Elaine Vickers
Illustration © 2023 by Ana Aranda
Book design by Laurent Linn © 2023 by Simon & Schuster, Inc.
SIMON & SCHUSTER BOOKS FOR YOUNG READERS and related marks are trademarks of Simon & Schuster, Inc.
For information about special discounts for bulk purchases, please contact Simon & Schuster Special Sales
at 1-866-506-1949 or business@simonandschuster.com.
The Simon & Schuster Speakers Bureau can bring authors to your live event. For more information or to book an event,
contact the Simon & Schuster Speakers Bureau at 1-866-248-3049 or visit our website at www.simonspeakers.com.
The text for this book was set in Fertigo Pro.
The illustrations for this book were rendered in watercolor, ink, gouache,
colored pencils, and watercolor pencils on watercolor paper.
Manufactured in China
1222 SCP
First Edition
2 4 6 8 10 9 7 5 3 1
Library of Congress Cataloging-in-Publication Data
Names: Vickers, Elaine, author. | Aranda, Ana, illustrator.
Title: How to make a memory / Elaine Vickers ; illustrated by Ana Aranda.
Description: First edition. | New York : Simon & Schuster Books for Young Readers, [2023] | "A Paula Wiseman Book." | Audience: Ages
4–8. | Audience: Grades K–1. | Summary: Visualizes the various ways to remember and cherish life's most special moments.
Identifiers: LCCN 2022019313 (print) | LCCN 2022019314 (ebook) | ISBN 9781534494411 (hardcover) | ISBN 9781534494428 (ebook)
Subjects: CYAC: Memory—Fiction. | LCGFT: Picture books.
Classification: LCC PZ7.1.V533 Ho 2023 (print) | LCC PZ7.1.V533 (ebook) | DDC [E]—dc23
LC record available at https://lccn.loc.gov/2022019313
LC ebook record available at https://lccn.loc.gov/2022019314

Life is a little like the world itself:
always spinning along,
always moving forward.

All this spinning and moving
means that someday
something you love will come to an end
and it will be time to say goodbye.

When that happens, you will have
an important job to do:

REMEMBER

To remember means
to keep something in your mind.
To hold it safe in your memory,
like a small, smooth egg in your hand.

How do you make a memory?
And how do you remember?
Here are some ways.

Take a picture!
If you don't have a camera, you can draw it.
If you don't have paper, here's a trick:
You can take a picture
just by blinking.
All you have to do is close your eyes
at just the right moment
to save it straight to your memory.

Tell the story!
You can write it down
or say it out loud:
the funny parts,
the scary parts,
even the sad parts.
Any audience will do,
including just you.

Sometimes you will remember without even trying.
All it will take is
a few notes of a song,
or the scent of just the right something on the breeze,
and the memory is there, clear as the day it happened.

Sometimes your body keeps the memory for you:
the stretch—toes to fingertips—toward the highest shelf,
the still-there shadow of a scraped knee,
the feel of your fingers, snug between theirs.

Sometimes all you have to do to remember is
sit quietly,
breathe,
maybe close your eyes.
Listen.

And the memory comes back,
all at once
or sneaking up beside you,
warming you like sunshine,
soothing you like gently falling snow.

It might make you smile
or even laugh.

Sometimes remembering might make you sad,
and that's okay.
Sometimes some parts you won't remember.
And that's okay too.

Love is memory,
kind eyes and warm smiles,
familiar words in a familiar voice,
a feeling of being seen and safe.

When you are ready,
take all the memories—
the pictures and stories and all the rest—
and imagine them there inside you,
making you
YOU.

These memories will be there
in the moments you need them most,
giving you
hints and answers to new tests you face,
a compass for steering back to your truth,
or a good dose of courage from knowing
that you have been brave before.

With your mind full of memories,
you are ready
to go out into the world,
smart and true and brave and loved,
making new memories
making you even more YOU.

Sometimes the best way to remember
doesn't feel like remembering at all
but more like
spinning along,
moving forward.

So even when it's time
for something you love to come to an end,
your story goes on
and your memories do too.